Level 3

Spooky Night

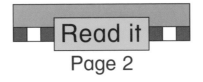

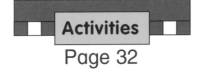

"Look out! That creepy one-eyed slime
monster is coming right at us!"
screamed Jack.

"Yikes!" cried Billy. "That thing is bigger than Alaska!"

After the movie ended, Jack said to Billy, "Wow! That was the best scary movie ever!"

Read it

"Billy? Where are you, Billy?" Jack looked all around the basement for his brother, but Billy was gone!

"Oh, no!" thought Jack. "What if Billy fell into a deep black hole and the slime monster is eating him for dinner?"

"Or what if a huge, hairy bigfoot stepped on my brother and squished him like a pancake?"

"Or maybe a creepy giant hand reached out from the sky and grabbed Billy up into outer space!"

Jack was very scared. Where did Billy go? Then he heard footsteps ...

It was BILLY! "Where were you?"
asked Jack. "I just had to go to the
bathroom," said Billy. "I hope you
weren't scared without me."

"Oh, no—not me," replied Jack. "I wasn't scared a bit."

Look at the picture on each page, and then write the story in your own words.

There

Write it

"Look out! That creepy one-eyed slime monster is coming right at us!" screamed Jack.

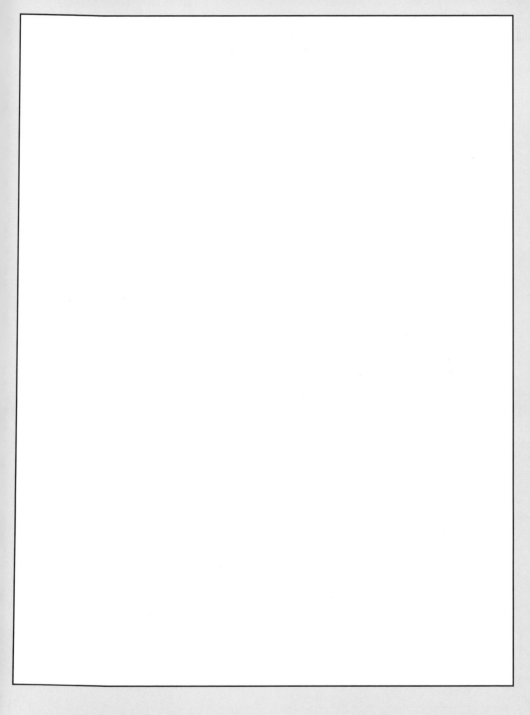

"Yikes!" cried Billy. "That thing is bigger than Alaska!"

After the movie ended, Jack said to Billy, "Wow! That was the best scary movie ever!"

"Billy? Where are you, Billy?" Jack looked all around the basement for his brother, but Billy was gone!

"Oh, no!" thought Jack. "What if Billy
fell into a deep black hole and the slime
monster is eating him for dinner?"

Draw it

"Or what if a huge, hairy bigfoot stepped on my brother and squished him like a pancake?"

"Or maybe a creepy giant hand
reached out from the sky and grabbed
Billy up into outer space!"

Jack was very scared. Where did Billy go? Then he heard footsteps . . .

It was BILLY! "Where were you?" asked Jack. "I just had to go to the bathroom," said Billy. "I hope you weren't scared without me."

Draw it

"Oh, no—not me," replied Jack. "I wasn't scared a bit."

Activities

Read it:

Say something! For this activity, choose a Now I'm Reading!™ book and place five to ten sticky notes throughout the pages. Next, have your child or student read the book aloud to a family member or friend. Whenever he or she gets to a sticky note, he or she should say something about what he or she thinks of the story or the characters, what he or she wonders about what may happen later in the story, what he or she connects with in the story, and so on. This is a super way to make an emerging reader think about what he or she is reading to improve comprehension skills!

Write it:

Write the news! Have your child or student find an interesting headline from the local newspaper. He or she should cut the headline out with scissors and glue it on the top of a blank piece of paper. Next, he or she should write a story to go along with the headline. Encourage him or her to be creative and zany! Your child or student can even create his or her own newspaper by gluing various articles together onto an extra-large piece of paper!

Draw it:

Complete a picture! Have your child or student find a picture from a newspaper or magazine. He or she should tear the picture out and then cut the picture in half with scissors. Then, he or she should glue one half of the picture onto a blank piece of paper. Now your child or student should try to draw the missing half of the picture next to the existing half of the picture. He or she can try to make it look real—or very silly!

A NOTE TO PARENTS:
When children create their own spellings for words they don't know, they are using **inventive spelling**. For the beginner, the act of writing is more important than the correctness of form. Sounding out words and predicting how they will be spelled reinforces an understanding of the connection between letters and sounds. Eventually, through experimenting with spelling patterns and repeated exposure to standard spelling, children will learn and use the correct form in their own writing. Until then, inventive spelling encourages early experimentation and self-expression in writing and nurtures a child's confidence as a writer.